# A CHILD'S BOOK
## *of*
# BLESSINGS

*For Sophie and William, the major blessings in my life — S. D.*
*For Megan and Ben, with all my love — O. W.*

Barefoot Poetry Collections
*an imprint of*
Barefoot Books
37 West 17th Street
4th Floor East
New York, New York 10011

This book is printed on 100% acid-free paper
The illustrations were prepared in watercolor and ink
on 140lb watercolor paper

Graphic design by Jennie Hoare, England
Typeset in Cochin 16pt
Color separation by Tien Wah Press (Pte) Ltd., Singapore
Printed in Hong Kong/China by South China Printing Co. (1988) Ltd

1 3 5 7 9 8 6 4 2

U. S. Cataloging-in-Publication Data

Dearborn, Sabrina.
   A child's book of blessings / compiled by Sabrina
Dearborn ; illustrated by Olwyn Whelan.—1st ed.
[40]p. : col. ill. ;    cm.
Summary: A collection of blessings from a variety of
countries and cultures: blessings for times of the day
and for the seasons, for activities and journeys, and
for loved ones.
ISBN 1-84148-010-X
1. Prayers--Juvenile literature. 2. Meditations--Juvenile literature.
I. Whelan, Olwyn, ill. II. Title.
291.43/ 2 --dc21   1999   AC   CIP

# A CHILD'S BOOK
## *of*
# BLESSINGS

compiled by
## SABRINA DEARBORN

illustrated by
## OLWYN WHELAN

BAREFOOT BOOKS

# Contents

# Contents

# Introduction

A BLESSING IS A SPECIAL KIND OF PRAYER. When we offer a blessing, we allow a sense of the sacred quality of life to flow through us. We can also use blessings to express that experience in a way that touches others.

Children carry a blessing quite naturally. They possess a natural sense of wonder and curiosity about life. Their spontaneity and pleasure in things creates an infectious joy.

As we grow older, it is important that we develop ways of keeping our awareness of the sacred flowing through everything. It is also important that we pass on this awareness to children.

Many of our traditional customs and beliefs are designed to help us to remember the sense of wonder we experienced when we were young. They also help us as families and communities to pause and feel the goodness in life and the many inner and outer blessings that we share. However, a blessing can be performed by anyone; you do not have to subscribe to a particular religious tradition. Taking time to give and receive a blessing creates an endless flow of love. What you believe is secondary; the sincerity with which you act is what counts.

It is very easy to give a blessing to a person, an animal, an object or a place. When you bless someone or something, you open your heart and mind to let good thoughts and love flow through you.

These vibrations of love and good will are absorbed by whoever receives them.

To give a blessing, imagine a sense of peace within and around you, inside and outside. Then sit or stand still and think loving thoughts and feel loving emotions. Let those thoughts and feelings travel through your body and into your heart and then out through your hands. Gently hold your hands, palms down, over any object and imagine the love flowing into that object. You can also send a blessing to those around you by imagining the love radiating from your heart like a big, happy sun or a beautiful flower opening to release its fragrance.

We often give blessings without even thinking about it. A house that is well cared for has a nice feel to it. Pets who are loved are friendlier and happier. Teddy bears and cuddly toys receive lots of love, and even when they are worn out and old, they have a warm, magical feel about them. If we can give blessings without thinking of it, just imagine how much more powerful those blessings can be when we take the time to slow down and concentrate on them.

The blessings in this book are prayers that can be said at special times to help us pause and acknowledge the energy of the universe flowing through us. They are ways of acknowledging that we are blessed and can pass this blessing on to others, especially our children.

*Sabrina Dearborn*

# Blessing for
# Those That You Love

God bless all those that I love.
God bless all those that love me.
God bless all those that love
those that I love and all those
that love those that love me.

*from a New England sampler*

# Morning
# Blessings

At night make me one
with the darkness.
In the morning make me one
with the light.

*Wendell Berry*

10

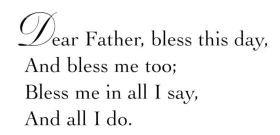

Dear Father, bless this day,
And bless me too;
Bless me in all I say,
And all I do.

*Elfrida Vipont*

11

# Blessing for Peace

*P*eace to you from my heart to your heart.

*Sufi*

12

# Blessing
## for Protection

*B*e thou a bright flame before me,
Be thou a guiding star above me,
Be thou a smooth path below me,
Be thou a kindly Shepherd behind me,
Today, tonight, and forever.

*St. Columba of Iona*

# Blessing for a Newborn Baby

*A* small wave for your form
A small wave for your voice
A small wave for your speech
A small wave for your means
A small wave for your generosity
A small wave for your appetite
A small wave for your wealth
A small wave for your life
A small wave for your health
Nine waves of Grace upon you.
Waves of the Giver of Health.

*Celtic*

15

# Blessing to Start an Activity

*C*andle Fairy burning bright,
come and share with us your light.
May we always learn to share
with the children everywhere.
Candle Fairy burning bright,
come and share with us your light.

*Steiner*

# Blessing to End an Activity

*M*ay the Circle be open,
but unbroken.
May the love of the Goddess
be ever in our hearts.
Merry meet and merry part
and merry meet again.

*Starhawk*

# Mealtime
# Blessings

*T*he bread is pure and fresh,
The water cool and clear.
Lord of all life, be with us.
Lord of all life, be near.

*African*

Give thanks to the Mother Earth.
Give thanks to the Father Sun.
Give thanks to the plants in the garden
Where the mother and the father
      are one.

*Steiner*

Blessed are you, Lord our God, King of the Universe, who brings forth food out of the earth.

*Jewish*

21

# House Blessings

*B*less this house O Lord we pray.
Make it safe by night and day.

*Christian*

*B*lessed is the spot, and the house,
and the place, and the city,
and the heart, and the mountains,
and the refuge, and the cave,
and the valley, and the land,
and the sea, and the island,
and the meadow where mention
of God has been made
and his praise glorified.

*Bahai*

# Water
# Blessing

*W*aters of Life
Pour forth
upon our thirsty world.

*Christian*

24

# Fire
# Blessing

Remember, remember
the sacredness of things
Running streams and dwellings
The young within the nest
A hearth for sacred fire
The holy flame of fire

*Pawnee*

25

# New Year Blessing

*M*ay you have success in
all endeavors.
May you have peace and health
in the four seasons.
May your happiness be
as wide as the sea.
May all your comings and goings
be peaceful.

*Chinese*

# Blessing
## for all Life

*B*lessed are you, Lord our God,
King of the Universe, who has kept us
alive and supported us and brought
us to this season.

*Jewish*

# Blessing
## from the Stars

*W*e are the stars which sing.
We sing with our light.
We are the birds of fire.
We fly over the sky.
Our light is our voice.
We make a road for the Great Spirit.
Amongst us are three hunters
who chase a bear.
There was never a time when
they were not hunting.
We look down on the mountains.
This is the song of the stars.

*Passamaquoddy*

# Blessing for a Journey

*M*ay the road rise up to meet you.
May the wind be always at your back.
May the sun shine warm upon your face,
The rains fall soft upon your fields.
And until we meet again,
May God hold you in the
Palm of His hand.

*Irish*

# Halloween
# Blessing

$A$t this time of dark and night,
spirits often give a fright.
We call upon the ancient dead,
circling now around our head.
Bring the blessings from before,
while we stand with open door.
Ancient spirits hear us now,
peace and love do we avow.

*Sabrina Dearborn*

# Christmas Tree Blessing

*L*ord our God,
the heavens are the work of Your hands,
the moon and stars You made;
the earth and sea,
and every living creature came into being
by Your word
and all of us too.
May this tree bring cheer into this house
through Jesus Christ,
Your good and holy Son,
who brings life and beauty to us
and to our world.
Lighting this tree, we hope in his promise.

*Rev. Victor Hoagland, C.P.*

# Bedtime Blessings

*G*od, that madest earth and heaven,
Darkness and light;
Who the day for toil has given
For rest the night;
May Thine angel-guards defend us,
Slumber sweet Thy mercy send us,
Holy dreams and hopes attend us,
This livelong night.

*Bishop Heber*

Great Owl of Dreams,
Wings soft and furred with dark,
Soar through my sleep
To that tender place between
the eyes and heart.
Bring me the dream in your mother beak,
The dream to feed me and teach me
and guide me,
Great Owl of Dreams.

*from*
***Celebrating the Great Mother***

Four corners to my bed,
Four angels around my head.
One to watch and two to pray,
and one to keep all fear away.

*Jenny Dent*

# Resource List

## FESTIVALS

*A Calendar of Festivals*, Cherry Gilchrist, Barefoot Books, Bath, UK, 1998.

*Festivals Together: A Guide to Multi-cultural Celebration*, Sue FitzJohn, Minda Weston and Judy Large, Hawthorn Press, UK, 1993.

*Celebration! Festivals, carnivals and feast days from around the world*, Barnabas and Anabel Kindersley, Dorling Kindersley Books, UK, 1997.

*World Wide Crafts Celebrations*, Chris Deshpande, A&C Clark, London, UK.

*Festivals in a Multi-Faith Community Celebrations*, Cecelia Collinson and Campbell Miller, Edward Arnold, a division of Hodder & Stoughton, London, UK, 1989.

*Themes for Early Years Spring & Summer Festivals*, Carol Court, Scholastic Ltd, UK, 1997.

*Festivals Resource Pack*, Bill and Lynn Gent, BBC Educational Publishing, London, UK, 1995.

*Festivals and Saints Days — A Calendar of Festivals for the School and Home*, Victor J. Green, Blandford Press Ltd, UK, 1979.

*Festivals, Families and Food*, Diana Carey and Judy Large, Hawthorn Press, UK, 1982.

*Festival Year Calendar*, a large wall poster available from NES Arnold Ltd, Educational Supplier, Ludlow Hill Road, West Bridgeford, Nottingham, HG2 6HD, UK.

*Celebration*, series by A&C Black, London, UK: Dat's New Year, Diwali, Eid ul-Fitr, New Baby, Sam's Passover.

## WORLD RELIGIONS

*World Religions*, David Self, Lion Press, UK, 1996.

*A Wealth of Faiths*, Joanne O'Brien, Martin Palmer and Ranchor Prime, World Wide Fund for

# Resource List

Nature Education Department, UK, 1992.

*Religions of the World* series by Wayland Publishers Ltd, UK, 1986: Islam, Buddhism, Judaism, Sikhism, Hinduism.

*The Family Wicca Book*, Ashleen O'Gaea, Llewellyn Publications, USA, 1994.

*Celebrations of the Great Mother*, Cait Thompson & Maura P. Shaw, Destiny Books, USA, 1998.

*Ritual, Power, Healing and Community*, Maladoma and Patrice Some, Arkana, Penguin Books Ltd, UK, 1995.

*The Celtic Tradition*, Caitlín Matthews, Element Books Ltd, UK, 1989.

*Dharma Family Treasures: sharing Buddhism with children*, edited by Sandy East Oak, North Atlantic Books, Berkeley, California, USA, 1994.

## PRAYERS AND BLESSINGS

*A Child's Book of Prayers from many faiths and cultures*, compiled by Tessa Strickland, Barefoot Books, Bath, UK, 1997.

*Earth Prayers From Around the World: 365 prayers, poems and invocations for honouring the Earth*, edited by Elizabeth Roberts and Elias Amidon, Harper, San Francisco, USA, 1991.

*The Puffin Book of Prayers*, compiled by Louise Carpenter, Puffin Books, UK, 1988.

*A Little Book of Celtic Blessings*, Caitlín Matthews.

*My First Prayer Book*, Treasure Press, UK, 1988.

*Reflections of Pearls*, Inam Uddin & Abdur-rahman ibn Yusuf, Prudence Publications, UK, 1996.

*Christmas Prayers and Customs*, Rev. Victor Hoagland, C.P., The Regina Press, New York, USA, 1997.

# Credits & Sources

BAREFOOT BOOKS publishes high-quality
picture books for children of all ages and
specializes in the work of artists and writers
from many cultures. If you have enjoyed
this book and would like to receive
a copy of our current catalog,
please contact our New York office —
Barefoot Books Inc., 37 West 17th Street,
4th Floor East, New York, New York 10011
e-mail: ussales@barefoot-books.com
website: www.barefoot-books.com